LET THE WRONG ONE IN

JS HARKER

CONTENT DISCRETION

This work contains bondage, discipline, and sadomasochism. There will be blood and rough play. The cornerstone of healthy BDSM is "Safe. Sane. Consensual." The action between the two characters is consensual, but as they are supernatural beings, what is safe and sane for them has a slightly different definition. Vampires in this world setting do not need to breathe, and they heal incredibly quickly. This alters masochistic play for them and is not meant to accurately reflect real life. This work is meant to be fantasy and entertainment.

In other words, don't do this at home. Unless you're somehow a couple hundred year old vampire and a motorcycle-riding werewolf.

CHAPTER 1

Rain splattered against Gabe's helmet as he steered his motorcycle onto the road leading farther up the mountain and into the richest part of Taliville. Darkness enveloped him, the only blips of light coming from the mansions of the elite—and mostly vampiric—residents of the sleepy supernatural town. Taliville didn't have much in the way of streetlights. It didn't need them. With almost half of its seven thousand citizens having some supernatural lineage, most of the town saw fine in the dark.

Gabe was a werewolf and had little trouble seeing the road ahead of him. Even if his vision had been worse, he was certain he could've made this drive. He knew Taliville inch for inch. He'd been through its streets, grown up in its forests, and helped build some of its homes. Taliville wasn't just in his blood; it was his bones.

And he wasn't going to let some outsiders and a pompous-ass vampire ruin what his family had spent generations creating.

The rumble of his motorcycle was a steady echo of the tumbling of his rage around his mind. His pack, the

Gealach Dearg, was the oldest pack in Taliville. Nell might've declared the town a supernatural sanctuary, but the wolves had made it a safe haven when there was little more than a couple of houses and a vampire's idea. Gabe's family had built most of the damn town. Literally.

Recent years had seen booms and busts, and thanks to a rival pack moving in and making waves, the Gealach Dearg kept losing business that should have been theirs. The town was turning toward cheap instead of craftsmanship, wanting fast instead of good. Homes, small renos— didn't matter. The new pack kept underbidding Gabe's father and stealing the work.

Just when things looked bleak, they had landed a big job. Brand-new mansion for a vampire.

Only that little motherfucker had sent an email saying that he needed to "keep his options open going forward."

Gabe growled, a sound lost to the thrumming of his bike and the rain. His leather gloves creaked. He had to keep a lid on his anger, or he'd split his gloves and potentially damage his bike. Old lessons from his father played back, but thinking of his father and the broken way he'd been sitting at the kitchen table wondering how he was going to pay everyone next month only set Gabe off again.

Born a werewolf, Gabe had struggled with his multiple forms most of his life. Rage tended to bring out his inner beast, but not because the beast was feral. During his teenage years, Gabe had realized that being a wolf was far more freeing. Wolves were expected to growl and bite and snarl and snap at whatever stressed them out. They could run for miles in the woods and just exist. Humans had to behave. They had to be decent. Especially when over half the town was deeply invested in any gossip about them.

He pulled into the long driveway of his destination.

Starter homes for vampires in Taliville were the older houses that had been built back when the town was just young. Set back from the road, on a bit of a hill, the three-story structure had a charm that had lasted through the century it'd been standing. The architecture had been heavily influenced by a Victorian vibe rather than the Art Deco or Modernist movements that had been popular at that time. It always reminded Gabe of his grandfather, the son of the man who'd originally designed the place. It was formidable, not entirely unapproachable, but stern and stately.

Any bastard should've felt lucky to live in such a freaking beautiful historic home. But vampires always had to build new things to put their "stamp" on the world. So the prick currently living in the house wasn't satisfied with it anymore.

That was, in theory, fine. The vampiric need to build something bigger and grander put food on the fucking table.

But the gall the bloodsucker had in practically promising the job to Gabe's pack and then meeting with the other company drove a spike of hot heat into Gabe's heart.

The house was practically dark, but that didn't matter. Vampires were up all night playing their little mind games with mortals. Gabe was not in the mood to drive back home yet. If the vamp wasn't here, he'd wait for him.

He brought his bike to a stop underneath the overhang in front of the main door. The bike's vibrations continued to purr through him even after he turned the machine off. The sensation kept him rooted in his human form. He pulled his helmet off, tossed it down beside his bike, and then stormed up to the door. It was still the original oak that Gabe's great-grandfather had cut and polished himself. But it was a door made to take a beating, so he slammed his fist against it.

A deep, resounding crackle of thunder tumbled across the dark sky while he waited. Gabe clenched his jaw and his fists. A howl was in his throat and a snarl on his lips. He could give in and let some of the shift happen. His hybrid form would add on some height, lengthen his jaw, sharpen his teeth, give him claws. His hearing would improve, too. Despite the storm and excellent craftsmanship, he'd be able to hear inside the house, at least what lay just on the other side of the door. He'd be able to tell if anyone was coming closer or if he was being ignored.

He'd also wreck his gloves, possibly ruin his leather jacket, and his jeans would get real tight. And he *liked* these clothes.

Slowly, eventually, the door swung open. Just inside was a fair-skinned man with deep blue eyes and a petite frame. He wore a velvet blue robe that matched his eyes and accentuated his paleness and sharp, angular features. His light brown hair didn't have the luster that it might've had in bright light, but it came down to his shoulders in an artful, pretty way. His robe was tied at the waist, though he'd done it so his bare chest was on display. He had on silk sleep pants and a pair of slippers that matched his goddamn robe.

Collin was as dramatic as the rest of his kind. He'd dressed like he was playing some role in a perverted game, just like Gabe had figured he might. This act of being unbearably wealthy and completely at ease was like the start of a porno. The bastard leaned against the door, one hand holding on to it over his head. In his other hand, he had a glass of what smelled like Bronte Delight, a wine that Collin's fucking vineyards produced.

Seriously? What kind of rich asshole sat around drinking their own wine in a dark mansion on a rainy night and played freaking mind games with the locals?

Gabe's right glove started to split.

Collin raised one eyebrow. "Did you come to glower at me? Or do you have something to say, Gabriel?"

Five points for him that he knows the difference between me and Rafe. Minus fifty for being an obnoxious motherfucker. Gabe wasn't entirely surprised that Collin knew which Wheeler twin was which. Collin had been sniffing around Rafe for a couple of years. He likely knew the basics, such as Rafe didn't drive a motorcycle and Gabe did. He might even know that Gabe was right-handed where Rafe was left.

But the fact that he could pick them apart made Gabe a little more certain in his theory about why he was pulling the job away from his pack.

He ought to control his tone. He ought to be a business professional and keep this polite. His aunt wanted him to be lead contractor someday, and contractors needed to be able to handle bullshit minutia without letting their temper get the better of them. At least in public. In private, he could go run around the woods like a wolf and get the venom out of his veins.

But this little prick was causing problems, and there might not be a company if he got his way.

Gabe's voice was rough from anger and the undeniable impulse to let this bastard know he was seen for what he was: a manipulative pain in the ass. "I heard you were thinking of going with YWP."

A small smile tilted Collin's pale pink lips, and merriment brightened his eyes. "I may have made a few phone calls."

And the most infuriating, mind-fucking, messed-up thing was that in spite of every ounce of anger in his bones, Gabe felt his heart twinge with want when Collin smiled at him. He knew that vampires could induce desire or fear in others, that they sensed it like a wolf could sniff out a rabbit in the woods, but he'd been around blood-suckers enough to know when someone was screwing with his head. Vamps in Taliville tended not to do so without consent. Their coven master Nell forbade it. Between that and knowing his own emotions well enough, Gabe was certain Collin wasn't using his powers on him.

Collin was just Gabe's dream type. He was bordering on too waifish for reality—rumor was he'd been dying of consumption before he was made in the early 1800s—and was angular in a delicate way but in a could-cut-glass sort of way as well. And the attitude. He had such a fucking self-important demeanor and absolutely no-fucks-given sort of tra la la to his voice that made Gabe want to bend him over and make him cry in all the good ways that would wreck him for anyone else, at least as long as Gabe was alive. He itched to take hold of the vamp and etch himself into Collin's memory so that if the bastard managed to live until the sun blew up, he'd look back and go, *Ah, yes. Gabe. He was* magnificent.

But this was the first time Gabe had ever felt like Collin had seen him. In the meetings, Collin's gaze had always lingered on Rafe out of everyone else. Wasn't hard to conceive—Rafe was the prodigy who'd gotten his degree in architecture. He was going to be the one to design houses while Gabe built them. A lot of people picked Rafe over Gabe, and he tried not to let it bother him. Rafe was the golden child. Gabe was his shadow.

Getting mad at Collin for doing what everyone did wasn't fair. But he could get pissed if he was going to ruin the family business. He snarled, "You were going to go with us, and then all of a sudden, you're not. What gives?"

"Change of heart," Collin said smoothly. Then he started to shut the door.

Instinctively, Gabe slammed his hand onto the closing door and pushed. Collin only looked frail. He had a two-hundred-year-old vampire's strength, and he kept the door from opening further. So Gabe put more force behind his shove. The door swung free of Collin's grip and slammed into the wall. Gabe had seven inches of height on the guy and a hell of a lot more weight, but if they did get into a fight, the odds were in Collin's favor. Not by a lot, but by enough that Gabe wasn't about to underestimate the smart-ass.

"This really about looking at your options?" Gabe growled. "Or did you finally make a move and my brother said *no*."

Collin's lips twisted from a polite smile to a sly, devious one. In his maddeningly soft voice, he said, "I would *never* be so petty. YWP offered a better price."

"We've been bending over backwards researching and preparing our proposals. You've been bitching about quality, and we've been meeting the demands. And on the eve of signing the paperwork, you want to pull out?" Gabe sneered down at Collin. "I'm calling bullshit. This ain't about price."

"Not all of you have been 'bending over,'" Collin replied.

"So this is about Rafe." Gabe took a step closer. When Collin took a step back, a crackle of joy went through him.

Rafe was the good twin. The one with the kind smiles that made people all gooey and the genuine heart that listened to everyone's troubles. He was the one who could sigh and have folks of all genders crawling all over him to fix his problems.

People sometimes thought that Gabe was like him. That because he shared Rafe's red-blond hair, blue eyes, and muscular physique, they had to share temperaments. They assumed he was the same. Kind to a fault. Caring.

But sometimes, a wolf needed to feed his pack. Sometimes, a snap of the jaws fixed things that a gentle nuzzle never could. He growled and took another step toward Collin. "What will it take?"

This time, Collin didn't back up. He laughed quietly, bringing his hand up to cover his mouth like an aristocrat of bygone years.

Gabe kept his fists at his side. Ripping the bastard's heart out certainly wasn't going to land him the contract. Getting on his knees and begging wasn't in his nature. His gloves were starting to split. His control on keeping to his purely human form was slipping. Along his jaw, around his ears, and across his chest, his hair began to thicken. The rumble in his throat deepened in a way that soothed his need to growl without ridding him of any anger.

"Oh my, you are intense." Collin had such a soft voice, hardly above a whisper. The rain would've drowned him out if Gabe didn't have shifter hearing. He raised his hand to touch Gabe's cheek. "How did I miss that?"

Gabe snatched Collin's wrist and pulled his hand away from touching him. He glowered down at the vampire, who was all smiles and far too pretty. His guts flip-flopped as a deeper urge to claim rolled through him.

Thunder echoed into the hallway. Rain continued to splatter on pavement and forest out beyond the door. There was a wildness outdoors that Gabe relished, and the weather seemed to egg him on. To embrace what was lurking in his nature.

Collin made looking like a Victorian waif work for him. And there was an appeal in knowing that while the guy looked thin as a ghost, he could bench-press Gabe's bike easier than he could. And all of that only strengthened the growing urge to pin Collin down and claim him like the vampires had done to so many others in this small town.

Because really, nothing was ever *Gabe's*. Everything was the pack's or the family's—even his notoriety in town was shared with his twin.

All Collin would've had to do was pick the right twin, and Gabe would've come crawling to him.

But he hadn't. Instead, he'd played fucking mind games.

Some lesser werewolves would blame their inner beast for the urges rolling through Gabe, but beasts weren't vindictive with their claims. Gabe longed to itch the deeper instinct he'd rarely indulged. He wanted to make Collin *his*, to mingle their scents together so the whole damn town knew that Gabe was just as great a predator as any fucking vampire.

He was going to show Collin what a mistake he'd made in focusing on Rafe.

"You don't know the half of it," Gabe growled. "But you're going to learn."

CHAPTER 2

Collin laughed. He couldn't help himself. Mortal boys were so damn funny when they took themselves seriously!

Gabe was darling. Storming up to Collin's house in the middle of a thunderstorm on a motorcycle, of all things. Absolutely charming, in a hilarious way.

Of *course* Collin had anticipated such an action when he'd sent the email earlier. The Wheelers were doing their best to meet his demands and, quite frankly, were the better builders in town. But Rafe had stopped answering his texts, so Collin had to do something for attention.

The problem wasn't, as Gabe had phrased it, about Collin making a move and Rafe saying no. Rafe had said yes several times over the last couple years. And afterward, he would slink away and act like a guilty puppy until he crawled back to Collin for another night. Collin had thought that he'd finally push Rafe into becoming an item, but Rafe slunk off and ignored him. Ignored his texts.

What would Gabe say if he knew the whole reason Collin had launched the project of a new mansion in order to make Rafe talk to him again? Clearly, Rafe hadn't told anyone about their relationship. Which unfortunately tracked with the way Rafe had a habit of acting like every erotic turn they'd taken was not something to be proud of.

And yet, for all their time together, Rafe had never shown half the intensity Gabe currently had in his blue eyes. The few times he'd allowed any of his wolf nature to show had been a slipup he'd apologized for. Gabe was on his way to his half-human, half-wolf hybrid form, and there wasn't a hint of desire to keep the beast at bay or a fear of losing control, at least not of his wolf form.

And he was just so charming that Collin had to laugh. He was a delight!

"'But you're going to learn,'" Collin repeated, intentionally lowering his voice to mock Gabe. Then another laugh started to bubble out of him.

"You think I'm funny?" Gabe grabbed him roughly around the throat. Little pricks broke the skin of his throat where Gabe's nails had grown out into claws. He closed the distance, and Collin's wineglass hit the floor with a crash. Gabe's face was only inches from Collin's, and his breath stunk of beer, steak, and garlic.

Collin scrunched his nose. "I thought you were being cute, up until I smelled that breath of yours."

"Yours isn't a picnic, precious," Gabe said. His voice had taken on a growly timbre that was going straight to Collin's groin. "Old blood. Bad wine."

"Bad wine?" Collin sputtered. "Excuse you! My vineyard is amazing."

Gabe grinned slyly.

The little shit was trying to get a rise out of Collin. *Well, touché.* Collin lifted his chin defiantly. "Ha. Ha."

"Doesn't feel good when someone insults your work,

does it?" Gabe tightened his grip, forcing Collin's chin up even more. The wolf was already taller than him, but he'd grown another three inches. "Though I doubt you do much of the actual work."

Collin was up on his tiptoes. His slippers weren't designed for this sort of stance, and he was quickly having to hold on to Gabe's arm in order to keep his claws from digging in deeper. There was a delicious sort of fun in dancing on the edge of being ripped apart. Collin's sire had to be rolling over in his grave—as much as ashes could roll anyway. His sire had always preached to never give away an upper hand.

And yet, Collin couldn't resist a good twist of his wrist.

"More … than you might … think," Collin managed. Vampires didn't need to breathe, but they did need air to speak.

"Vampires don't work. They take. That's all they're fucking good at." Gabe squeezed just that bit tighter and moved in closer. He was radiating heat. His red-blond hair had grown shades darker to a beautiful auburn. What had been stubble along his jawline thickened into fur. His eyes blazed with faint blue light. "What if I took? Hm?"

Collin strained to get the air to speak, but Gabe wasn't budging. Without leverage, Collin would have a harder time breaking Gabe's grip. He formed a fist and lightly thumped on Gabe's chest. The move wouldn't even bruise Gabe temporarily, but that wasn't his intent. He wanted to test Gabe's resolve, wanted to see if he had what it took.

He had to know if he was wasting his time on another Wheeler twin or if he might finally find what he was looking for.

Gabe snorted at him, then snuffed in a big breath. His grin grew more salacious, and that rattled loose the butterflies in Collin's stomach. Leaning in, he pressed his nose against Collin's neck and inhaled. He rumbled in Collin's ear, "Didn't know vampires let off pheromones."

Collin grunted, still unable to speak.

Gabe traced a line down Collin's throat with his thumb, the claw delicately slicing skin along the way. "You know what you smell like?"

Collin knew. He was getting hard with the knowing. Still, he squirmed because doing so meant feeling Gabe up against him. And Gabe was—*unf.* Rafe had muscle left over from his high school football days, but Gabe had kept up with training, apparently. Shifting to his hybrid form wasn't enough to create the hard six-pack Collin felt through his thin T-shirt.

"*Prey,*" Gabe snarled into Collin's ear.

The way he said it sent a wondrous tremble through Collin. No one had treated him like this in over a decade. Finding a good wolfboy was hard work. Most shied away from him in the end. Thought he wanted too much, thought he was a bit too twisted. Or they were scared that they were monstrous for their desires like Rafe had been by the end.

Gabe was speaking with a confidence that Collin hadn't come across in years. That alone would have been enough to get him hard. Getting choked in his front hallway while the storm threatened to come in through the open door was just icing on a very rich cake.

Gabe took another deep inhale.

Then he threw Collin with grace and speed down the long open hallway. Collin sailed through the air, a moment of pure glee, before he made contact with the hardwood floor. He landed on his side and slid another three feet across the polished wood.

"One chance, rabbit," Gabe murmured. In the darkness of the hallway, his blue eyes blazed, and what little light bled from other rooms gleamed off his sharpened teeth. "The truth. Were you pulling the job to get Rafe's attention?"

Collin rolled onto his back so that he was propping himself up with his elbows. His libido was begging him to ignore sad and mundane things since he clearly had underestimated what a thrilling partner Gabe might be. Fun was preferable to pain.

With a smile, Collin rose to his feet. His robe had fallen open, so he let it slip off his shoulders and puddle on the floor. As much as Gabe seemed to be stepping into Collin's desired game, he could be playing his role hard enough to get the answer he wanted. He may want to rip Collin to shreds, no matter his answer.

When he met Gabe's stare again, he realized the wolfman was raking his gaze over the lines of Collin's body. He was no masterpiece, no fine work of art transformed into an angel of death like so many of his kind. Life had been a series of illnesses; his body had been a prison he could never escape. He was frail, too thin, and, frankly, annoyingly short in his own estimation. After two hundred years, he'd come to terms with his lackluster body. He knew how to dress to entice, how to manipulate the desires of his prey so that they truly enjoyed him.

Yet he hadn't worked any of his abilities on Gabe. The werewolf had caught him off guard, and their little exchange had been so exhilarating that Collin hadn't used any of his magic. He was prepared to, if need be, either drive Gabe from this house or trick him into a night of sex. Anything to ease the sting that Rafe's silence had left behind.

But he didn't need to. Gabe was a fireworks display of lust. Despite the quiet of the rain and passing thunder, tuning in to his desires filled the silence and created a symphony for Collin. As Gabe continued to let his gaze roam over Collin, the growly confidence remained. He *wanted* Collin, no magic manipulation required, and he had full control over his wolf side. What he was showing was what he wanted to show.

Collin stilled as he peered further into Gabe's wants and fears. So many mortals committed to one action when desiring another altogether. Too many of his lovers had woken up and regretted the act. Even if they came back, they were never comfortable. Never their true selves in the way he longed for very long. Once in a generation, Collin happened upon one, maybe two, that would be what he needed them to be.

Gabe wanted the job for his family's business. That was painfully obvious without digging into his emotions.

He had also meant what he'd said. *Prey. Rabbit.* He had the itch that Collin hoped they could scratch together.

Collin had already risked his heart on one Wheeler twin. He was chiding it for piping up in this moment. He wouldn't easily let another mortal in so soon. If they went through with what he badly desired, then he'd likely fall for Gabe worse than he had for Rafe.

Clenching his fist, he raised his chin. The spots of blood on his neck were already drying, the tiny wounds closed. As coldly and firmly as he could, he said, "I wanted my lover to notice me."

"*Lover,*" Gabe snarled. He started to drag in a breath.

Collin could feel his revulsion rising. He took one step forward and snapped, "I know he never claimed me. I know that what he and I did drove him from my bed. He could not handle what I asked of him. And I thought … I thought the job would bring him back to me. I thought I could pour honey onto our wounds and they would heal. But he refuses me."

"You and Rafe?" Gabe tilted his head. "You expect me to believe that?"

The confused wolfman was an amusing sight, but Collin was far from laughing. "Do you have a mole on your inner right thigh like him? Or is yours on the left since you're mirrored?"

CHAPTER 3

The question threw Gabe for a loop that circled the planet twice over before coming back to him. He'd seen his brother naked plenty. Sharing a room in their house, learning how to shift together, and being on the football team together meant they'd had no sense of modesty around each other. Yet he had to stop and think about that detail. Collin was right. Rafe did have one there. And Rafe was too shy of a shifter to change around anyone other than close family.

Meaning Collin was telling the truth. He and Rafe had slept together. Or Collin had really, *really* been stalking his brother.

But Rafe had been acting squirrelly lately. Ever since Collin's job had come to them, Rafe had been looking to ditch the project. He'd even seemed relieved when the email had come in earlier tonight. Had tried to call Gabe back into the bar when Gabe announced his intent to ride up here. Told him they didn't need to deal with that weirdo despite the fact that they desperately needed the job.

The vampire had been manipulative but not any worse than Gabe would've been in his position. Until a minute ago, Gabe had even been enjoying the strange, thirsty tension between them. Learning that Rafe had been hiding his connection to Collin rattled Gabe's confidence. His claws began to shrink back to his normal nails.

"Don't lose your edge now," Collin said flippantly. His seriousness melted away into a subtle bratty grin.

Anger wasn't hard to find. After all, this little prick was probably using him as a stand-in. Gabe growled, and his nails extended again. "You might not want to see my *edge*."

"Oh, but I do," Collin purred. "You are something rare, Gabe. I would wager you've had trouble feeling satisfied."

"I get off just fine," Gabe grumbled.

"You had your hand around my throat." Collin put his own hand at the base of his neck, and he shivered. The heady scent of musk colored his earthy grave scent. "How often do you do that to a lover?"

The answer was not often, but Gabe wasn't going to tell him that. Because the truth was he wanted to. But he could seriously injure other mortals, even other shifters. While shifters healed faster than humans, they weren't as quick as vampires. The undead immortals could just *take* more. More wealth. More time. More damage. Gabe had had more than a few fantasies about what he might do if he could get his claws into one. His fellow packmates talked about finding their soul mate and making babies and all those "pleasant" things.

He wanted to lay his claim on someone. Wanted them to be *his*. Wanted to mark his territory, spiritually at the very least.

Gabe peeled off his gloves and shoved them in his

pockets. Doing so wrecked the leather the rest of the way, which pissed him off more. Holding the place between his human form and hybrid became too hard. His shoulders broadened, and he hurried to take off his leather jacket before it was ruined. Hair sprouted all over his body and thickened into silky auburn fur. His jaws lengthened, and his teeth sharpened. Though his bones cracked, each pop was a burst of relief. His legs lengthened, giving him greater height as they morphed into wolflike haunches.

He dropped his leather jacket to the floor and tore off his boots.

Panting, he glared down the hallway at Collin. His hybrid form was what felt most natural, like he no longer had to hold half of himself at arm's length.

Collin had a sly, slick grin that Gabe wanted to own. The little vamp was a brat of the highest caliber.

The rage that had been boiling under Gabe's skin settled into a growl that he had a masterful hand on. He rolled his shoulders, feeling the seams of his Henley start to give. Shifting gave him clarity. He wanted things from Collin, but he was tired of placing hope on a pedestal. Toppling over again would break more than his heart.

"Careful, rabbit," Gabe said, his voice deeper and throatier. "I'll gnaw off your legs to get out of this trap you've set."

"That is wonderfully vivid but far too cryptic," Collin replied.

Gabe padded down the hallway toward Collin. The little vamp stayed where he was. Their height difference was even greater now, and Collin tipped his head up to keep his gaze locked with Gabe. "You toyed with us to get at *him*. Now, you're messing with me. I am not a consolation prize."

"You are very much the grand prize," Collin said, a note of reverence in his voice. He almost touched the center of Gabe's chest, but he stopped himself.

Vampires could lie. The only things in the universe that couldn't were faeries, and even they might dance around the truth until it no longer mattered. Pheromones were harder to fake. Hard-ons not impossible, but that took some body control greater than even Gabe had.

Collin's sleep pants were over his erection, hinting at his hardened length.

"The. Job." Gabe glared down at him. He snuffed, enjoying how the air rebounded off Collin.

"I only wanted a little bit of attention," Collin replied. "I was never going to hire the other company."

"It's ours?" Gabe demanded.

"*Yes*," Collin said with a sigh. "Now, have you been teasing me? Or are you interested in me?"

The promise that Collin wasn't going to give away the job released the angry stress in Gabe's shoulders. Being rid of that meant he could stop thinking with his big, responsible brain and start finding relief for the other itch building in him. Grinning was easier. He grabbed Collin's jaw in one hand and dug his claws in just a little as he forced him to tilt his head.

"I'm interested, rabbit." He took in deep sniffs, finding Collin's scent. Musk and earth and the faintest hint of lavender. "I'm in the mood for a hunt. Big house like this must have plenty of holes to hide in. Think you can run from the big bad wolf?"

"I can make you work for it," Collin said with the cockiest, most sinful smirk that Gabe had ever seen.

"Then *run*, little rabbit," Gabe murmured in his ear. Then he released Collin's jaw.

Collin flashed a broader smile at him, and then he took off into the house with a vampire's speed.

Counting to twenty took wasn't stressful. As much as he yearned for Collin, he wanted his little brat to have a chance to think everything through. Wanted to see how seriously he'd take the game. Because there was a chance that maybe, maybe, he would be his little brat for more than a night. And hope could let him down worse than anything. He wanted to let it linger a moment before reality had a chance to crush it.

But anticipation crawled up his skin, and he couldn't remain in hope's limbo. He finished his slow count, sniffed the air, and followed Collin's trail.

If Collin's heart could beat, he was sure it would be thundering worse than the storm outside. The wind and rain had picked up again, and the constant rumblings were covering up the other sounds in the house. Collin had two mortal donors—pets—and though he sometimes enjoyed sex with them, they were submissive types. He liked that in his pets.

Gabe promised to be something altogether different, and Collin had to use his restraint not to just strip down and have his ass up in the air begging for him. Gabe had said he wanted a hunt, and the mere suggestion of being chased made Collin's dick threaten to leak. The hunger in Gabe's growlier, hybrid voice was a narcotic that Collin needed to sink his teeth into.

No one had made him ache like this in decades. He was determined to make the fun last.

The house had three floors, a basement, an attic, and a converted stable that had been turned into a garage in the 1970s. Along with the typical staircases, there was an elevator at the back of the house, a dumbwaiter connecting the kitchen with the pets' quarters, and a few secret passageways on the second and third floors. He slipped behind one of the panels on the second floor that led into the space between rooms. The secluded hallway was narrow, but he was nimble and had no trouble navigating through the tight darkness.

Confident he had a clever hiding spot, he stopped at the corner instead of carrying on to another exit. His scent was all over the house. Gabe was never going to find him here. Once Collin figured he'd struggled long enough, he would emerge and be extra sassy.

The panel slid open a minute after Collin had settled in. He dipped around the corner as Gabe called out with a chuckle, "Little obvious, rabbit."

How had he known about the passage? Collin reached the other end and slipped out quietly into the next hallway. The house still had much of its original molding, and the sight of it reminded Collin of the history the Realtor had walked him through when he was purchasing it. One of the first mansions in Taliville, built and designed by the local pack.

Fuck me. His family built this place! The realization changed Collin's strategy. Gabe was stalking the hallway toward him, his footfalls just a bit more thunderous than the storm now. Collin opened the door of a guest room beside him. He bit into his hand and shook a few drops of blood into the room. Then he closed the door as quietly as he could and took off for the staircase.

Up would lead him toward his bedroom, one of his playrooms, nearer to the attic, and his private music room. Down were more common rooms—living room, kitchen, and the like—and the way to his sex dungeon in the basement.

Hesitating would give Gabe time to catch up. Collin hurried up the stairs.

Unless Collin braved the storm, there would be no escaping Gabe. That had never been the goal, but the knowledge finally sank into him. The game of a hunt was always how long until he was found, where the finding happened, and how the finding came about.

But if Gabe knew about a secret passage on the second floor, he likely knew the layout of the entire house. This would not be a long hunt.

I will still have my fun. Collin grinned. There were two ways to reach his walk-in closet where the ladder to the attic was. One went through his bedroom, the other through his upstairs playroom. He was tempted to let Gabe find him among the dildos, restraints, and myriad of other toys. However, he longed to know what Gabe would do if he found him somewhere else. Would he fuck him on the spot? Did he have more in mind than simple fucking? He seemed charged with predatorial urge to discipline Collin. Was he inventive? Or brutal? Could he be both?

Collin slipped through the playroom and through the door to his closet. Holding in a laugh, he pushed his large, heavy trunk in front of the door to block easy entrance. If Gabe tried to shove his way through, he'd have to break the door or the trunk to make enough space. The door from Collin's bedroom was unobstructed, but he hoped that having to go around would frustrate Gabe a smidge more. Gabe's growls were delectable.

Collin tugged on the rope, and the attic ladder glided down to him. Vampiric speed was handy, but he decided to move silently instead. He reached the attic and gently pulled the ladder back up. It folded into place nearly as silent as he had been.

The attic was a place of cobwebs that Collin's staff only cleaned out once a year entirely at his behest. When he'd thought of this as the perfect hiding place, he hadn't stopped to think about how much of his past was in the various trunks. Those older pieces of himself were behind the boxes of Halloween and Christmas decorations—Taliville had annual challenges, and Collin did not like being outdone by anyone other than Nell, the town's head vampire—but he glimpsed them between the stacks of cardboard.

Gabe was bound to be a one-night stand. Pulling him up here was like tossing a diary onto a desk in front of him. What if he became sidetracked? What if he fucked him with the shadows of his past all around?

I'm getting old if I'm thinking so much about that. Collin shook his head at himself and then made his way to the far end of the attic. The path was clear and the darkness near complete, even for his eyes. There was a light, but he wasn't going to do Gabe the favor of switching it on.

Instead, he slipped into his coffin. He hadn't climbed into it in nearly forty years, preferring the comfort of beds. The last time had been out of necessity. He hadn't moved into a new home, and his coffin was far safer than assuming the curtains in his hotel room would block the sun. The lid had a lock on the inside, but he didn't want his coffin ruined nor to send Gabe a message that he'd given up on the game.

Once the lid was down, Collin was utterly without light and the air wasn't moving around him. The smell was musty. Clearly, he needed to instruct his staff to air this thing out during their yearly cleanings. Perhaps more often than that. Just in case.

However, he was in a sort of isolation chamber. His

hearing could pick out a few noises, mostly the rumble of thunder, and his ability to sense fears and desires was curtailed more than he'd thought it would be. Typically, he could feel his pets anywhere in the house. He had only a dull sense of them at the moment, and Gabe was another dim blaze. Was it the coffin?

No. No, *he* was the problem. He was aching for Gabe to find him, and his own needs were too bright to see anything beyond them. His imagination was running wild with all the possibilities before him. Hope was a fire, threatening to scorch every defense and leave his heart open wide for Gabe to ruin.

This would just be sex. Nothing more. Plenty fun. But Gabe would never hold on to him. Why would he want to when Collin had nearly ruined his family?

Gabe was not as quiet when he pulled down the ladder, and he certainly didn't attempt to silence the way he climbed up into the attic.

There was nowhere else to run. Collin had been foolish. He should have tossed the wolfboy out instead of entertaining any night with him. Rafe had seemed eager to embrace his darker side, but he had pulled back. So many of the men Collin liked held back when he wanted them to continue. Every time he felt like he was on the edge of feeling alive again, they balked and walked away, never wanting to look his way again.

Losing Rafe's pretty face had been hard.

Losing Gabe, losing those pretty eyes, would devastate him. And they had barely touched.

Collin bit his lower lip, careful not to pierce his skin. What had he been thinking?

Gabe lifted the lid of the coffin. He'd turned on the light, but it was behind him, casting shadows over most of his features. He was every inch the wolfman that Collin longed to bend over for. "There you are, little rabbit."

Fuck, the way his voice was an aural aphrodisiac was just unfair. Collin was grateful he couldn't blush. As he started to sit up, Gabe grabbed him around the throat. His claws dug in, and he hauled Collin up.

The wolfman's dick was hard and *massive*. Collin had seen thousands of cocks in his long life and marveled at all of them. Gabe's was still bound by his tight jeans, but the fact that he was so hard, that he was grinning, only tightened the tension in Collin's heart. Chasing him around the house had encouraged Gabe, and that was fantastic.

Gabe dragged him over to the opening to the third floor. Rather than pushing him onto the ladder, he dropped him.

Collin had been expecting to put his feet on the ladder. He'd aimed one foot that way, and it caught. The tumble to the floor was rough. Bones broke. But as soon as they were snapped, they began to mend. He rolled with a soft groan and gave in to his body's instinctual need to move into a better position for his healing to work.

Gabe had intentionally hurt him. And he snuffed in a sort of chuckle up in the attic as he turned out the light.

The burning hope that maybe Collin had finally found the right one continued to blaze.

The ladder was made for human-sized creatures and not much for large beasts. Gabe climbed down, but it was not a graceful thing. When he reached the floor, he leaned down and grabbed Collin by the jaw again.

"You heal, rabbit?" Gabe asked, sniffing him.

"Yes," Collin whispered.

"You're not glaring. Not running. Not scared. Not outraged," Gabe commented. He tilted Collin's head back and licked his throat. "You taste horny, rabbit. You're a little masochist, aren't you?"

Gabe's claws dug a little deeper when he finished his question. The bits of pain around Collin's jaw were nice. He wished some mark of what Gabe would do to him would stay, but his healing was already pushing at Gabe's claws, ready to heal him as soon as the intrusions were gone.

"Yes," Collin murmured.

"Oh, the fun we're gonna have," Gabe said in his ear, his tone quiet and bordering on worshipful. "You're going to call me wolf, got it?"

Collin grinned slyly. "Once you earn it."

Gabe's smile grew wider, sharp teeth showing. "That's how you're going to be about it?"

"Yep."

"Awesome." Gabe grabbed him around the throat again, tighter than before, and dragged him out of the closet and into the playroom. "Noticed the setup in here, and got to say, I'm impressed. For a second, thought this was all so you could fuck your little pets, but then I got looking at it."

Though he attempted to dig his heels in, Collin didn't have a prayer at finding purchase against the floor in his bare feet. He clutched onto Gabe's wrist and arm. Doing so put him in contact with Gabe's buff muscles, and that sent a thrill through him. There was just something about being tossed around by a burly werewolf that was intoxicating.

Gabe dropped him onto the floor in the center of the room. Collin hadn't prepared for that and fell flat with a soft "Oof."

"This room's not for fucking them, is it?" Gabe padded over to the Saint Andrew's Cross and flicked one of the straps loose so that it dangled down. The silver studs glinted in the light. As he spoke in his growly voice, he ran one claw down the length of the X toward the center. "From size and silver, it's for *you*. You like to play the big bad predator out there, but you're a sucker for a wolf, aren't you, rabbit?"

Collin rolled over onto his stomach. Covering his nervousness, he shot Gabe a slick grin. "Maybe I like petite men."

Gabe snorted, a loud huff of sound that was a bit endearing. "I can practically smell your erection."

Collin laughed. "Did you think that line would work?"

"You're such a little brat." Gabe stalked toward Collin. Instead of stopping at him, he continued on to the cabinet.

Normally, it was locked, but Gabe must have picked it earlier because he swung it open without difficulty. Collin turned back over and sat up. "Excuse you!"

"Had to make sure this didn't hold any traps for me." Gabe winked at him. "Interesting stuff in here. Lube, dildos, and butt plugs, of course. Iron manacles. Whips? In a room this size? Too freaking small, rabbit. Think there's a silver cock cage, which is a choice. And then there's this."

Gabe pulled out a spray bottle.

Collin was glad he didn't need to breathe.

Sly grin growing, Gabe padded over and got down on his haunches to lean into Collin's face. "There's a little cross on this, rabbit. The silver, that could be for vamps or shifters. This?" He shook the bottle in Collin's face. "This is just for vampires. For *you*."

The last time Collin had encouraged a partner to use the holy water, his partner had been appalled at how much he'd loved the burn and pain of it. For all of Gabe's talk, he had only been talk so far. A little roughing up hardly counted between supernaturals like them.

But holy water was on the tamer ends of Collin's desires. If Gabe wasn't willing to really dig deep, then Collin didn't want to waste more than a night with him.

"You're a major masochist, aren't you, rabbit?" Gabe whispered, his voice low and warm with glee. He stroked Collin's shoulder with the tip of the spray bottle.

You're a fucking freak, Rafe had said in their last fight. Collin had been pushing that out of his head. He'd been worried that Gabe's voice would be too close to Rafe's, but he wasn't. It was like they played different keys on the same piano. Rafe had been full of sharp, bitter notes, especially once he loathed how far he'd gone to please Collin.

Gabe had a dancing lightness in his voice and a bold, mellow command adding to the harmony. He was gorgeous, and if Collin went through with this, he might lose himself.

But God above and the Devil below, Collin *longed* for someone to reach through and scratch that impossible place in his soul. He could never reach it on his own.

Holding Gabe's gaze, Collin placed his hand on top of Gabe's on the spray bottle. He maneuvered it to aim against his shoulder with less than a centimeter of distance.

Then he squeezed it.

The blast of holy water dug straight through his skin. The pain burrowed into him, and Collin arched, head tilting back. It was exquisite. It knocked away any worry, any concern. All too soon, it was dulling. The skin healing. But for a split second, he'd been out of his own head and in that place between ecstasy and agony.

When he opened his eyes and brought his gaze back to Gabe's, he braced himself for the rejection.

Gabe had awe in his wolfy face. Slowly, his expression started to morph, not to disgust but to excitement. He flashed a wide, sharp smile at Collin. "All right, rabbit. You want to see how far down I can chase you?"

"Yes," Collin hissed with want.

Gabe grabbed him roughly by the jaw and then kissed him. Their tangle of lips and teeth and tongues was a disaster of nicks, cut tender flesh, and drops of blood. Collin fucking loved it for all its sloppiness because Gabe was eager. Eager to hurt him. Eager to try to give him what he needed. Just *eager*.

When Gabe was done, he panted, warm breath coating Collin's cheek. He grabbed Collin's arm with his free hand and stood. Collin came with him but barely put any strength into holding himself up. That didn't seem to bother Gabe. His wolfman was so fucking strong Collin's weight was nothing to him. Collin would have swooned if he hadn't been doing that already.

His heart didn't stand a chance. But that would have to wait. Pleasure was bound to come first, and oh, he needed his wolfman to live up to his hopes.

CHAPTER 5

"Let's get you on the cross, rabbit," Gabe said. He yanked Collin forward toward the Saint Andrew's Cross. "Don't want you running on me."

Gabe dropped the spray bottle of holy water off to the side as he pushed Collin up against the cross. Trailing him through the house had been fun. When he'd stepped into this room the first time, he'd reflexively rubbed his hand down his hard cock. Along with the cross, there was a flat, full-sized bed against a different wall. The bed had the most basic of white sheets on it and the thinnest of pillows. Collin had a chair with plenty of straps and no real seat to it off in another corner. One cabinet had the toys that Gabe had mentioned, but he'd also opened the other two in the room. One was full of a variety of weapons—everything from wooden bats to short swords. The other had a bona fide fucking machine folded up and tucked away.

The problem wasn't finding something to use with Collin but choosing what to do to him. The way he had gasped and rolled his eyes back when the holy water had jetted into his shoulder had Gabe harder than he'd ever been in his life. Their kiss had felt clumsy, but Collin had a dreamy look in his eyes. Gabe wanted to push him further and keep him there until they both couldn't take it anymore.

He yanked Collin's sleep pants off and threw them off to the side before binding him to the X at both ankles and wrists. He tapped the center of Collin's chest with one claw. "Test it for me."

Collin clenched both fists and pulled against the restraints. He hardly put effort into the attempt, and Gabe thought he saw the wood threaten to bend. *Should build him something better.*

"Good, rabbit," Gabe murmured as he dug his claw into the center of Collin's chest.

Collin gasped and arched into his piercing touch.

Oh, the wicked, wicked ideas that were propagating like bunnies in Gabe's mind. He half wanted to shred his jeans off and masturbate in front of him. Just make him watch how he had wound Gabe up.

But there were so many things to do and that seemed far too tame.

Gabe scooped up the spray bottle. The first time, he'd barely had a chance to see what it had done to Collin's skin. He fumbled with the control on the nozzle to turn it more to a mist. The plastic wasn't designed for manipulation by someone with claws. But he managed it and squeezed the trigger. A gentle plume brushed against Collin's skin.

Instantly, his pale skin turned bright red. He let his head fall forward, brown hair tumbling down to hide his features, and moaned.

Annoyed that he'd missed the blissful face, Gabe growled and stepped forward. His claws snagged on Collin's hair as he grabbed him and yanked his head up. "I want to see how you like it, rabbit."

Collin grinned with a soft slyness. "Okay."

Oh, God, Gabe was going to remember that smile for the rest of his life. "Don't drop your chin this time."

"Okay."

Gabe released him and took a step back. He sprayed holy water on Collin again.

This time, Collin let his head fall back, chin going toward the ceiling, as he groaned. His chest turned bright red again, but Gabe still didn't get to see him lose it with the pleasurable pain.

"You little brat," Gabe growled. He swapped the setting back to a stream. He grabbed Collin's jaw and dug in his claws to force him to open his mouth. Then he shot holy water straight into the back of Collin's throat.

Collin's eyes glowed red and went wide. Vampires cried bloody tears, and tiny pinpricks of blood welled at the corners of his eyes. He coughed once, twice, and Gabe released his jaw so he could spit and hack. Doubt flared in Gabe, cold and sharp against the warmth of his joy. After another moment, Collin dragged in a ragged breath and raised his head. "Do it again."

The way Collin's soft voice was filled to the brim with lust shot straight into Gabe's veins. He nearly obeyed that wish. But he hadn't meant for Collin to like it that much. He'd meant to teach him a lesson.

"No," Gabe said firmly.

Collin whined in a needy, medium pitch.

"Nuh-uh."

"Please, wolf," Collin said.

Hearing the endearment tumble off Collin's lips was exactly as glorious as Gabe had hoped. It also reminded him that he was the predator here. He would decide. With a smile, Gabe swapped the setting to mist once more. He thought about seeing if Collin had a silver dagger, but he didn't need a sharp weapon when he had his claws. He put the spray bottle in his left hand.

"You need to learn a few things, rabbit," Gabe replied. "Your manners are awful."

Collin snorted. "Going to grab a paddle?"

"No." Gabe spritzed Collin's chest, nailing a bulk of his intended canvas in one spray. Collin's skin brightened.

Just as it started to fade, Gabe used his index finger claw to slice words into Collin's skin. He started at his left nipple, went to his right, and then a second line on his abdomen. *I will listen.* By the time he was done, Collin had bitten his lip hard enough to draw blood, and a small tear had slipped down one cheek. The first cuts were already healed. Remnant drops of blood remained, though some were sliding down Collin's skin.

"What did that say?" Gabe asked.

"Say?" Collin only half frowned. A gauziness had settled into his still-glowing red eyes.

He was gorgeous.

"Missed it? Guess I'll have to do it again. Got to clean the slate first, though." Gabe licked the drops of blood off Collin's chest. In his wolf form, he liked to eat his prey now and then. Collin's blood was different. It had a zing to it that left the lightest buzz on Gabe's tongue.

He scored Collin's skin again, though he added a little extra just above Collin's cock. *I will listen to wolf.*

"Did you catch it that time, rabbit?" Gabe nuzzled Collin's ear.

"I … I will listen to wolf," Collin replied slowly.

"Good boy." Gabe licked his cheek. He tossed the spray bottle aside. With his thumb, he drew two short lines on Collin's inner thigh as he spoke. "Now that was twice. We're going to do it three more times so you remember."

Collin whimpered and bit his lip harder. He was muffling his moan.

"Bratty rabbit likes being punished, doesn't he?" Gabe rumbled as he started slicing into Collin's skin. He pushed a little deeper than he had before. An itch long held in the back of his mind began to unwind as he continued.

"Yes," Collin groaned.

Gabe etched a third slash onto Collin's thigh. The first two were gone, but the point was made. He began again. "Figured. But you're going to behave for me."

"Uh-huh." Collin gasped when Gabe made an especially deep N. "Oh, God. Need you."

"Shush. I'm not done yet." Gabe finished the fourth round. The blood was starting to make Collin's chest slick, so he took some time to lick him clean. Collin arched up toward him as much as he could. Gabe grabbed his hips, digging his claws in, and shoved Collin's ass back against the cross.

Then he went for the fifth.

Pretty tracks of tears crawled down Collin's cheeks. He had cut his lip with his fangs a few times, but he didn't hang his head. With long, ragged breaths, he moaned while Gabe worked. When Gabe was done, he whined in a high, begging note.

"Cock," Collin pleaded.

"Not yet." Gabe sniffed Collin, drawing in every note of his scent. Collin was worked up, and somehow, that made him smell even more delicious than normal. "Thought of something else you need to learn."

Collin pouted.

Gabe nipped his lip, which made Collin squirm.

All of Collin's haughtiness was ripped away. He was relaxed against his bindings, letting his wrists do the bulk of the work to hold him up. The silver studs in the straps had to be burning him, but he was clearly where he wanted to be.

Gabe had given up art years back. He hadn't been good at it, but fuck if he didn't want to take some pics of Collin for reference.

"Next lesson," Gabe rumbled. He carved his next phrase down Collin's chest and then added the last two words to either inner thigh. *I will hide better next time.*

"Write it again," Collin sobbed.

"What did it say?" Gabe asked.

"I know. I know. I wanna feel it again." Collin locked his gaze with Gabe. "Please, wolf. *Please.* Write it again!"

He was fucking undone in the best ways. Gabe needed to feel him around his dick sooner rather than later. Tormenting Collin, driving him into this sobbing, beautiful mess, was all Gabe's doing. No one else had been part of it.

"Since you asked so nicely," Gabe breathed. He cut the words into Collin again, going deeper.

The red wounds lingered, a sign that Gabe had been pushing Collin's healing ability. Not that Collin seemed to mind. Multiple streams of tears coasted down his cheeks, and he was starting to drool, all while his eyes fluttered and he moaned. He was handsome and darling and ridiculously cute at the same time.

Gabe was so fucking hard. "One last phrase, bunny. Then you'll get my cock."

"Yes, yes, yes. Do it." Collin puffed up his chest, creating a larger space to write.

Gabe almost took him off the cross right then, but Collin was so ready to take the words that Gabe couldn't deny him. Slowly, a little more carefully, he cut in the words *Gabe's Bunny*.

"'Gabe's Bunny,'" Collin murmured. "Mean it. Tell me you mean it!"

"I mean it, bunny." Gabe undid Collin's ankle bindings first. Then he wrapped his arm around Collin and undid the first wrist strap.

He'd started to fear that Collin was a little too far gone, but as soon as Collin's wrist was free, he dropped his hand to Gabe's waistband. Though he fumbled, Collin was dedicated to getting Gabe's jeans undone.

"Hold on a second," Gabe grumbled.

"I want your cock, wolfie," Collin mumbled, nearly an incoherent mess of words.

Any reservation Gabe had about holding back vanished. He undid Collin's other wrist, more careful because he didn't want to accidentally sever Collin's hand off than caring for the strap, and then swept Collin up and over his shoulder. He carried him across the room to the cabinet with lube. As much as he wanted to just shove inside him, his cock wasn't going to get far without a little help.

Then he took Collin and the lube over to the bed. He slung Collin down onto the firm mattress and tossed the lube next to him. "Spread some on your hole."

Immediately, Collin grabbed the lube and started to go to work. His attempts were sluggish and clumsy. He was getting plenty in the right vicinity, though, and he had his legs open wide, feet braced on the edge of the mattress and knees in the air.

He was just too damn pretty. His sobbing had slowed to soft hiccupping sounds, but drool was still leaking out of the corner of his mouth.

Gabe struggled to peel his jeans off. He tended to wear pants that had a bit of stretch in case he partially shifted, but these jeans had been his going-out pair. He'd been hoping to get lucky before he'd heard about Collin's email and driven up here. Getting the jeans off in one piece wasn't going to happen.

Shredding them off actually brought some relief. He hadn't realized how badly they'd been restricting him. Shame about losing them and his underwear.

Collin's look of needy awe mutating into wanton desire was worth having to tear his jeans. Gabe grinned down at him and put a clawed hand on either of his knees. "How long do you think you can hold out?"

Collin whimpered. His cock was already leaking beads of precum onto his stomach.

"Don't worry, bunny. I'm not going to stop until we're both satisfied." He shot Collin a wolfish grin.

With a thunk, Collin dropped the lube onto the bed beside him and reached for his own cock.

"Hey there, don't want you going too fast." Gabe gathered Collin's wrists into one hand and held them tight. He used his other hand to hold Collin's hips down while he began to push into him.

"Ah," Collin moaned. It sounded like it was supposed

to be a word, but it lacked any semblance of other syllables.

Gabe wasn't going to last long either. He managed to work his way into him. Collin's skin was cool, his ass only marginally warmer, and the tight cold was a balm against Gabe's overheated skin. Sinking into him was a mix of relief and need. He released Collin's wrists in order to chase his urges. Digging his claws into Collin's hips again, he began to pump into him in short, harsh strokes.

The mess of moans and whimpers bleeding out from Collin's lips drove Gabe to thrust harder and harder into him. Long bursts of come splattered out from Collin and coated his stomach, sprayed Gabe in the chest, and nearly caught Gabe in the eye. The long, shuddering moan that came after twisted Gabe's heart, and his cock began to thicken at the base.

He got in before his knot formed. Collin moaned in a throaty, subconscious-driven way, and his ass tightened all the more.

All Gabe could do was rut. He went onto his elbows over Collin, and Collin answered by throwing his arms loosely around his shoulders.

"Come in me, wolfie," Collin murmured in an ecstasy-laden voice.

Orgasm exploded through Gabe, and he bit into Collin's shoulder to keep from screaming out a howl. The sound came anyway, muffled against Collin's cool flesh.

Bliss had never been this fucking good.

Long moments passed before Gabe started to return to himself. Collin was limp against the bed, not breathing. A spike of panic started before Gabe remembered that Collin didn't need to breathe, so duh, of course he wasn't. He rubbed his finger through the blood on Collin's shoulder. The bite wound was healing, which was good because that meant Collin was fine, just worn-out. But Gabe did kind of wish that he could mark Collin as his so everyone would know.

Gently, Gabe stroked Collin's long hair and nuzzled him. His knot was still in place, only having gone down a little. He wasn't in any hurry, though. And his bunny would need some care.

CHAPTER 6

Collin was dimly aware that he'd been moved from one room to another, but he didn't rise toward full consciousness for a little while longer than that. When he did, he realized he was warm, which was a bit unusual, and then that he was in a bath. The water explained the warmth. He had been in it long enough for the heat to sink into his bones.

And he wasn't alone in the tub. He stretched and wiggled his backside up against Gabe. He was going to know the scent of that wolfman no matter what form he was in. At the moment, judging from Gabe's hands and arms that were wrapped around Collin, he was in his full human form.

God, the memory of Gabe in hybrid form growling and thrusting his hips was going to make Collin hard again. Languidly, he let his hand drop down to his cock and gently begin to stroke.

"You wake up and that's the first thing you do?" Gabe chided in his ear. He slid his hand under Collin's and laced their fingers together.

"Hey," Collin complained. His voice felt rough. That happened so rarely and was a little unpleasant. He'd healed from the shot of holy water in his throat—truly an inspired move on Gabe's part—but he had been crying and vocal. Gabe's ministrations must have left him weak, hindering his healing capabilities, and Collin's tonsils hurt.

He tensed.

"Something wrong?" Gabe asked tenderly.

"My throat." Collin put a hand at the base of his neck and tried to quell the panic building in him. He wasn't sick. He wasn't fucking mortal. "It's rough."

"Might have overdone it with the holy water," Gabe murmured.

"No. That was great." Collin's voice cracked. "I just ... I need a little blood. Just a little. Kyle is—"

"Not coming anywhere near this tub." Gabe held up his left forearm. "Here."

Collin didn't hesitate to sink his fangs into Gabe's arm. He hated the sandpaper feeling in his throat. As soon as Gabe's sweet blood touched his tongue, he began to heal. After a few mouthfuls, he wasn't only healed but refreshed.

That only happened with a deep connection. Collin hugged his torso tight, one hand still linked with Gabe's and the other lightly touching his side under the water. Hoping he might have even a chance at what he longed for was too much.

"You still smell worried," Gabe said.

"You can smell worry?" Collin asked.

"Mm, deflecting?" Gabe nuzzled behind his ear. He kissed him there, all warm breath and smooth lips.

"I'm waiting for the other shoe to drop," Collin replied.

"What other shoe?"

Better to rip open a vein than to have Gabe rip out his heart in the future. Slowly, Collin rolled over so that he faced Gabe. And Gabe, for his part, coaxed Collin to straddle his lap, which was wonderful and terrifyingly intimate. What they had done had laid Collin bare, but this tender moment threatened to strip every defense he had left. He had to know if he needed to repair them. Had to know if he was letting the flame of hope burn too brightly.

Gabe was smiling softly at him, and his blue eyes had the same warmth the rest of him had. Collin rested his hand on Gabe's chest, over his heart, and let his steady rhythm calm him. All signs tried to tell him he was being paranoid, but he wasn't willing to risk the not-knowing.

"I adore what we shared," Collin said tentatively. He dared to meet Gabe's gaze.

Gabe raised an eyebrow. "You trying to kick me out?"

"No!" Collin slid the last few inches forward so that he was pressed chest to chest with Gabe. The tub was slick, and he started to slide away, but Gabe looped an arm around him and locked him in place. He ran his hand through his hair so that it would stay out of his face. "I loved what you did to me. It was amazing. *You* were amazing."

Gabe's smile broadened, and he was radiantly handsome. "Good."

"You're ... not ... what do mortals say these days? Freaking out?" Collin asked.

"Why would I?" Gabe stroked Collin's cheek.

Collin leaned into his touch but frowned. "I've had lovers balk after the fact."

"Because you're a major masochist?"

Collin nodded.

Gabe narrowed his eyes. "Is my brother one of those

who freaked out—don't answer that. I'm not interested in his sex life. Not with you naked on my lap like this. Look, I'll admit that was the first time I've ever really scratched that particular itch in myself, but I had it something bad. Feels like I've actually found some relief."

"Relief?" Collin echoed.

"That and more." Gabe's grin turned mischievous. "Watching you submit like that? I mean, thinking about it has me, well, I think you can tell."

Collin could feel Gabe's cock between his legs, and he was harder than he'd been a moment ago. Nervousness flipped to excitement, and Collin slid his hand down to reach for Gabe's dick. His own was trapped between their abdomens, pressing against Gabe's firm, warmer skin.

"You liked slicing into me?" Collin asked.

With an affectionate light in his eyes, Gabe smoothed a stray strand of Collin's hair back and then caressed where Collin's jaw met his neck in slow circles. "Do you remember the last words?"

Collin trembled with hope made manifest. He stroked Gabe slowly, deliberately, and Gabe grew thicker, harder in response. "Gabe's bunny."

"Exactly." Gabe nipped at his chin, then lightly kissed him. "Watching you ride that pain and knowing you were wanting more was just too damn *right*. I had to claim you."

"Claim me?"

"I'm a werewolf," Gabe said, his voice oozing with liquid heat. "We can be *very* territorial."

"That so?" Collin smiled.

"Yup." Gabe drifted his hands down and cupped Collin's ass. He began teasing his hole, stretching him carefully.

The warm bath had brought a new sensitivity to

Collin's skin, which he hadn't realized until Gabe started to push a finger into him. He moaned, eyes closing reflexively, and rocked down onto his finger. "Tell me I'm remembering right. Tell me you knotted inside me."

"I did."

"Do you do that every time?"

"Mm, I have a feeling it'll happen more often than not with you, bunny." Gabe licked his jaw and nipped at him. "Want to find out?"

"Yes."

AFTERWORD

Hey there, reader peep! I'm so thrilled you took the time to read *Let The Wrong One In*. This story was a spicy blast to write.

In addition to my novels, you can find more of my work on Patreon including new serial stories!

Thanks for reading!

JS Harker

(PS reviews nurture muses and muses nurture writers and nurtured writers pen a lot more stories ;))

ALSO BY JS HARKER

The Fang and Dagger Saga

Wrong Hunt

Vicious Waltz

Wicked Games

Tit For Tat Series

Tit For Tat

His Fairy Prince

A Midsummer Night's Party

Also

Keep Me Safe

Soul Bond

ABOUT THE AUTHOR

JS Harker loves stories. She was one of those kids who constantly had a book in her hands and spent countless hours adventuring with her siblings. These days she wanders into her imaginary worlds and conjures up tales of magic, passion, and happily-ever-afters. She currently lives in the part of the Midwest that makes Tatooine look interesting by comparison (not that she's ever obsessively thought about becoming a Jedi or anything).

Follow her on Facebook or go to www.jsharker.com and sign up for her newsletter to receive updates!

Want more of her stories *now*? Be sure to join her Patreon!

www.ingramcontent.com/pod-product-compliance
Lightning Source LLC
Chambersburg PA
CBHW011146070726
47591CB00015B/2301

* 9 7 8 1 9 5 9 1 4 6 0 7 0 *